MIGHTY MORPHIN POWER RANGERS™

RITA'S REVENGE!

By Rusty Hallock

A PARACHUTE PRESS BOOK

GROSSET & DUNLAP • NEW YORK

A PARACHUTE PRESS BOOK
Parachute Press, Inc.
156 Fifth Avenue
New York, NY 10010

Published by Grosset & Dunlap, Inc., a member of The Putnam &
Grosset Group, New York. GROSSET & DUNLAP is a trademark of
Grosset & Dunlap, Inc. Published simultaneously in Canada.

Creative Consultant: Cheryl Saban.

With special thanks to Cheryl Saban, Sheila Dennen, Debi Young, and
Sherry Stack.

Printed in the U.S.A.
May 1994
ISBN: 0-448-40832-5
C D E F G H I J

The Battle Begins

Long ago, Good and Evil met in a great battle. The wizard Zordon led the forces of Good. He fought against Rita Repulsa, who wanted to rule the universe with her forces of Evil.

Both sides fought hard, but the war ended in a tie. So Zordon and

Rita made a deal. They would both flip coins to decide who was the winner. Whoever made the best three tosses out of five would win. The loser would be locked away forever.

Of course, Zordon did not want to risk the safety of the universe on five coins—unless they were magic coins! So with his five special coins, Zordon won the coin toss. But Rita had one last trick up her sleeve. Before she was locked away, she trapped Zordon in another dimension. Now he must stay inside a column of green light at his command center forever and ever.

Rita and her wicked friends

were dropped into an intergalactic prison and flung through space. They crashed into a tiny moon of a faraway planet. After ten thousand years, space travelers found the prison and opened it. Rita and her servants, Baboo, Squatt, Goldar, and Finster, were free!

Rita hadn't changed one bit in ten thousand years. She began planning to take over the universe again. And she saw her first target in the sky above—Earth!

When Zordon heard of Rita's escape, he put his master plan into action. He called Alpha 5, the robot running his command center on Earth. "Teleport to us five of the wildest, most willful humans in the area," he commanded.

"No!" Alpha 5 said. "Not... teenagers!"

But Alpha 5 did as he was told, and teleported five teenagers to the command center.

"Earth is under attack by the evil Rita Repulsa," Zordon explained to the teenagers. "I have chosen you to battle her and save the planet. Each of you will receive great powers drawn from the spirits of the dinosaurs."

Zordon gave each teenager a belt with a magic coin—a Power Morpher! "When you are in danger, raise your Power Morpher to the sky," Zordon instructed. "Then call out the name of your dinosaur and you will morph into a mighty fighter—a Power Ranger!

"Jason, you will be the Red Ranger, with the power of the great tyrannosaurus," Zordon explained. "Trini will be the Yellow Ranger, with the force of the saber-toothed tiger. Zack will be the Black Ranger, with the power of the mastodon. Kimberly will be the Pink Ranger, with pterodactyl power. And Billy will be the Blue Ranger, backed by the power of the triceratops."

For big problems, the Power Rangers could call upon Dinozords—giant robots they piloted into battle. And if things got really tough, the Dinozords could combine together to make a super-robot—a mighty Megazord!

Power Rangers, dinosaur spirits, and robots—together, these incredible forces would protect the Earth.

But the teenagers had to follow Zordon's three rules:

1. Never use your powers for selfish reasons.

2. Never make a fight worse—unless Rita forces you.

3. Always keep your identities secret. No one must ever find out that you are a Mighty Morphin Power Ranger!

CHAPTER 1

"Maybe she's in here,"
Kimberly said to her friend Trini.

The two teenagers dashed into the crowded gym at the Angel Grove Youth Center. It was full of kids practicing for the upcoming junior karate competition.

Kimberly dodged a karate kick,

and bumped smack into two guys. They were her friends Jason and Zack.

"Hey, what's up?" Jason said, adjusting the black belt of his karate uniform. "You look like you lost something."

"Not something," Kimberly said. "Some*one*. A twelve-year-old girl named Maria."

"Who's she?" Zack asked.

"We signed up to be her volunteer big sisters for the day," Trini answered.

"Cool," Zack said. "But where is she?"

"That's a good question," Trini answered. "She was with us a minute ago."

"Well, that's Maria," Kimberly said. "She can't sit still for more than a second."

"We have the greatest day planned for her, too," Trini said. "We're going for a picnic in the park. Then we're taking her to the new mall."

"I'm really getting worried. You don't think she's in some kind of trouble, do you?" Kimberly asked, nervously twirling a strand of her shoulder-length brown hair.

"How much trouble could a little girl get into?" Jason said.

Just then they heard a scream...then another. The shrieks were coming from the girls' locker room at the end of the hallway.

"The girls need help!" shouted Trini. She and Kimberly dashed into the locker room.

"Hey, who turned off the hot water?" a voice called out from the showers.

"I'm freezing!" another voice yelled.

"If I know Maria, I'll bet she has something to do with this," Kimberly said.

Kimberly and Trini peeked around a corner in the shower room. A little girl with long pigtails had her hands on a knob marked "Hot Water Valve."

"Maria!" Trini cried.

A big, silly grin spread across

Maria's face.

Kimberly shook her head. "Come on, Maria. Turn the hot water back on."

Maria did as she was told, while Trini brushed some drops of water from her long black hair. Then Trini led the way back into the gym. "We want you to meet Billy, Zack, and Jason—our best friends," Kimberly said to Maria.

Of course, there was something she didn't say. The five shared more than friendship. Trini, Kimberly, Jason, Zack, and Billy had secret superpowers that they used to fight Rita Repulsa, an evil empress from another world.

The three girls found Zack,

Billy, and Jason showing some new kick moves to a karate student.

"Hey guys, this is Maria," said Trini.

When Maria had met everyone, Kimberly turned to her and said, "Maria, we're not really angry, but why did you turn off the hot water?"

"I don't know," Maria answered slowly. "I guess I just wanted to get your attention. But now you probably don't want to be my friends."

Kimberly and Trini glanced at each other and smiled.

"Maria," Kimberly said, "you have our attention. Just be yourself. We'll be your friends no matter what you do."

"You will?" Maria said.

"Definitely!" Kimberly replied.

"You can count on us,"Jason said. Billy and Zack nodded.

"Hey, speaking of friends, I've got to go meet someone on the mat," Zack said. He was a black belt in karate. He taught a martial arts class for twelve-year-olds. Today his best student, Cameron, was going to compete. Billy and Jason were going to watch from the bleachers.

"Catch you later," Kimberly said as she, Trini, and Maria headed toward the door. "We're going to the park."

Meanwhile from her fortress on the moon, Rita Repulsa spied on the Power Rangers. She clutched her magic telescope with her long, pointed fingernails. Rita loved pointy things. The sleeves of her red and gold gown hung down in sharp points. The collar around her neck had sharp points, too. And on her head, she wore a crown of two pointed cones. Everything about Rita looked dangerous.

"Ha ha!" Rita laughed, as she watched the teenagers. "The Power Rangers are through! I've discovered the source of their power!"

Rita clapped her hands and

Finster came running. "At your service, Your Badness," he said. Finster was one of the evil creatures who served Rita. Finster was able to make monsters out of clay. Then he put them into his Monster-matic machine. It turned the clay into living, evil flesh.

"Finster, follow me!" Rita said. In a flash, she and Finster were transported to a cave on Earth.

The cave was cut into a steep cliff above the ocean. It was dark and muddy inside. The glow from Rita's deadly magic staff lit the way.

"Where are we going, Wicked One?" Finster asked.

"There!" Rita said, pointing to

the deepest, darkest part of the cave. A beautiful ancient treasure chest sat in a puddle of murky water.

"What is it?" Finster asked.

"You dweeb!" Rita shrieked. "Don't you know? That is the chest of the Power Eggs! And when I get them, all the power of the universe will be mine! Fetch them at once!"

Finster moved forward quickly. He couldn't wait to open the chest and grab the eggs. But when he touched the chest, a jolt of electricity flew through his fingers. He jerked his hand back in pain.

"Ow! Yeow!" Finster cried.

"Go back…back…back," a deep voice echoed through the cave. "Only a child of innocence may open the magic chest."

"An innocent child?" Rita screamed. "But where will I find an innocent child?"

She threw her arms in the air and made two fists. She stomped her feet. Her eyes narrowed into two scary slits, and she bared her teeth.

Then all of a sudden, Rita stood perfectly still and smiled.

"I know," she said with a wicked grin. "I'll just kidnap a little girl. I'll get that little brat Maria!"

CHAPTER 2

Back in the gym at the Angel
Grove Youth Center, the karate
competition was about to start.
The stands filled up with people.
A huge red and black banner hung
from the ceiling. It said: "Junior
Martial Arts Competition Today!"

Zack paid no attention to the

crowd. His warm brown eyes were focused on the boy in front of him.

"Hey, Cameron, try this," Zack said. Zack flipped on a music cassette. Then he went through a series of cool moves. He swung his legs in the air, then spun around in a dance move. Zack called this kind of karate Hip-Hop-Kido.

"Are you sure you want me to try that?" Cameron said.

"Absolutely," Zack said. "Trust yourself. That's what the martial arts are all about."

Cameron tried the Hip-Hop-Kido moves. He looked powerful and graceful at the same time.

At the very end, though, he lost his balance. He fell on the mats, landing on his back with an *ooomph!*

"Pretty close," Zack said encouragingly. "With a little more practice, you'll be great."

"But I don't have time to practice," the blond boy said. "The karate competition starts in a minute."

"That's okay," Zack said. "You don't have to do these moves for the competition."

Just then Bulk shoved his way through the door. Wherever Bulk went, he caused trouble. Today his friend Skull and his cousin Biff were with him. Biff looked just like Bulk. Both had stringy uncombed hair, scowls on their faces, and very large stomachs.

Biff signed in for the karate competition. Then he, Bulk, and Skull walked over to the mats where Cameron and Zack stood.

"Hey, Zack," Bulk said, "my cousin Biff is going to crush your wimpy dude!" He and Skull laughed.

"Grrr!" Biff growled at Cameron.

Cameron's eyes widened as he stepped back.

"Put your dog back in its cage, Bulk," Zack said. Then he leaned over and whispered to Cameron, "Don't let Biff freak you out just because he's bigger than you."

At that moment, Cameron's name was called over a loudspeaker. It was his turn to compete.

"I can't do it," Cameron said.

"Hang in there!" Zack encouraged, pushing Cameron toward the blue mats. "I'll be right in your corner if you need me!"

But then, the communicator on Zack's wrist started beeping. Zack knew it was a message from Zordon, the wizard who had given the five teenagers their superpowers. He was trying to prevent Rita Repulsa from destroying the Earth.

"Rita has sent the Putty Patrol to Earth to kidnap Maria!" Zordon said. "Kimberly and Trini need your help. They're in the park!"

"Oh, no, not the Putties," Zack thought. The Putty Patrol was Rita's fighting force of mindless clay creatures.

"Zordon, I can't go now. I promised Cameron that I would stay with him."

"Sorry, Zack," Zordon apologized, "but you're the only one I can reach. I can't signal Billy and Jason. They're in the bleachers. There are too many people around them."

Zack jumped up and shouted to Cameron, "I've got to leave! It's an emergency!"

"No way!" Cameron yelled.

"You can't leave! I'll never win the match without you!"

"Believe in yourself," Zack called back. He gave Cameron a look that said, *I'm sorry,* just as the bell to start the match rang.

Then Zack ran out the door.

The last thing the Power Ranger heard was the thud of Cameron hitting the mat behind him.

CHAPTER 3

As soon as Zack was outside the youth center, he touched a button on his teleporter wristband.

"I'm outta here," Zack said.

A moment later, a streak of light flashed upward and Zack disappeared into the sky. Almost instantly he reappeared in the park near Kimberly and Trini.

"Zack! What are you doing here?" Kimberly asked.

"Nice of you to drop by," Trini kidded. She held out a piece of fried chicken to Zack.

"You've got some uninvited guests," Zack said. "Look!" He pointed toward the trees behind Trini.

Kimberly, Trini, and Maria turned around and saw six gray creatures coming toward them.

"Putties!" Trini cried.

"Look out!" Zack shouted as the Putties headed for them.

"Oh, great," Kimberly said, taking a look at her pink shorts and white top. "Just what I need, Putty slime! I washed these clothes yesterday!"

One of the Putties came whirling in Kimberly's direction. She backflipped out of the way. Then she jumped up and kicked another Putty in the chest.

"Ki-yaaah!" Trini yelled. With lightning-quick speed, she flipped two more Putties to the ground.

Zack tried his Hip-Hop-Kido on the Putties. He did a flying leap through the air and planted both feet on a Putty Patroller's chest. The Putty fell down, did a backward somersault, and then jumped up again. The other Putties jumped up, too, and fought on.

Then two of the clay creatures grabbed Maria by the arm.

"Help! Help!" Maria cried.

Zack, Kimberly, and Trini spun around. Maria was being dragged into the forest by the Putties!

Before the Power Rangers could save Maria, the other four Putties charged them again.

"Maria!" Trini shouted. She tried to run and help, but the Putties flipped Trini over their shoulders and knocked Kimberly and Zack to the ground.

Then all at once, in a puff of smoke, the Putties disappeared— taking Maria with them!

CHAPTER 4

Kimberly got up from the ground and brushed pieces of grass from her pink shorts.

"This is the worst," she said. "We were supposed to be taking care of Maria. Now Rita's got her!"

"But why would Rita want to

kidnap an innocent kid?" Trini asked.

"I don't know," Zack said. "But I think Zordon knows. He called me and sent me to the park because he *knew* Maria would be kidnapped."

"Let's go back to the youth center," Kimberly said. "We need Billy and Jason's help."

The Power Rangers didn't waste any time. They touched the teleporter buttons on their wrist communicators. Like streaks of lightning, they were teleported back to the youth center.

The three Power Rangers ran inside, looking for Billy and Jason.

Bulk, Skull, and Biff show up at the karate competition ready for a fight.

Kimberly and Trini have fun at the park—but Putty trouble is on the way!

A Putty leaps in to attack!

Zack gets ready to teleport to the park to help Trini and Kimberly.

Zack tries his Hip-Hop-Kido on the Putties.

The Power Rangers' friend Maria has been kidnapped! They must find her— fast!

Kimberly tries to reach Zordon, but her teleporter won't work!

Billy's Rad Bug can travel to the command center in seconds!

The Power Rangers listen carefully as Zordon explains why Rita has kidnapped Maria.

Trini takes on a Putty outside the cave where Maria is being held!

The Power Rangers call on the mighty Dragonzord to help them defeat Rita's evil force!

The Power Rangers win again! Now it's time to find Maria!

The karate competition was still going on in the gym. Zack heard the announcer say that Cameron had won three fights. That meant he was in the final match!

Just then Cameron grabbed Zack's arm. Trini and Kimberly ran ahead into the bleachers.

"Zack! You're back!" Cameron said, his voice full of relief. "It's time for the final match—the most important one! Now that you're here, I know I can win it!"

"I'm back," Zack said, "but I can't stay for the match."

"Oh, man, but you promised!"

"I know," Zack said. "And I'm really sorry. But there's something I have to do."

Cameron's face fell. "You don't care what happens to me today," he said.

"I care, man," Zack said, "but you can't win if you're trying to do it for me. Do it for yourself. That's what counts."

Zack tried to give Cameron a high-five. Cameron pulled his hand away.

"I won't win," he said, walking away.

Just then Kimberly, Trini, Billy, and Jason came running up.

"Kimberly just told us about Maria," Billy said, slightly out of breath. "Let's get to Zordon fast. He'll know how to help us."

Once again, Zack gave Cameron a look that said, *I'm sorry*. Then he and his friends slipped out of the gym. They were going to teleport to Zordon's command center.

"Teleporting," Jason said.

He touched his teleporter. Nothing happened.

"What's going on?" Billy asked, frowning behind his glasses. He touched the teleporter on his wrist. Nothing happened.

"I don't believe it," Trini said. "Mine worked a few minutes ago."

"Oh, no!" Kimberly cried. "We're stranded! How will we ever save Maria?"

Everyone looked at Billy.
Billy could build or fix anything.
He was a whiz at science. He
used a lot of big words and tech-
nical terms when he talked.

"What do you think?" Trini
asked Billy.

"Something is blocking our teleporting signal. Repairs could take hours," Billy said.

"So what are we going to do?" Kimberly asked. "How will we get to the command center?"

"Well," Billy said slowly, "we could use my brand-new Remote Activated Drivingzord for Basic Ultra Geomorphology."

"Say it in English, Billy. Please," Jason said.

"Yeah, Billy," Kimberly agreed. "What is it?"

"It's a car!" he said, letting a smile spread across his face.

"A car? No way," Jason said.

"Yeah. Forget it, Billy," Zack said. "The command center is too far. It's out in the middle of the desert. We'll never get there fast enough in a car."

"We will in this one," Billy said. "Come on!"

The Power Rangers raced the few blocks to Billy's house. Inside the garage, they saw the car he was talking about. It was small and shaped like a beetle, with all kinds of gadgets and electronic parts attached.

"Meet the Rad Bug," said Billy.

The Rad Bug didn't look fast, but it was. It was able to go from zero to three thousand miles per hour—in three seconds!

"Buckle up, everybody," Billy said. "Here we go!"

Jason and Zack had barely

buckled their seat belts when a huge power field surrounded the car. It felt to Trini as if she were being pulled through time and space.

"This is one wild ride!" Zack shouted. "Better than being on a roller coaster."

"Whoaaah!" all the Power Rangers cried out at once.

A second later the Rad Bug screeched to a stop outside the command center.

"Awesome ride, man!" Jason said when he caught his breath.

"Yeah, but does it have a CD player?" Kimberly asked.

"Hey, Billy, what does this button do?" Zack asked.

"Zack, please don't touch that—it shoots the super cannon. Don't touch anything on the control panel, okay?" Billy said. "Zack? No, Zack! No!"

But Billy was too late. Zack had reached out and pushed a button.

BOOM!

Something exploded inside the Rad Bug's dashboard. Smoke poured out from the control panel. Sparks flew.

"Oops," Zack said in a meek voice. "What was that?"

"That, Zachary, was my microwavable lunch," Billy answered.

"Mmm. Macaroni?" Zack asked, sniffing the air.

"It used to be," Billy replied as he looked at the tray of black glop.

Everyone laughed. Then they squeezed out of the small car and dashed into the command center. Zordon was there. An image of his pale face wavered in a column of eerie green light.

"Greetings!" said Alpha 5, the robot who ran Zordon's command center. Red lights on his metal head flashed as he watched the Power Rangers.

"Hi, Alpha," said Jason. Then he turned to Zordon. "Zordon, we've got trouble."

"Major trouble," Kimberly added. "Rita has kidnapped Maria!"

"Calm down, Power Rangers," Zordon said. "I am aware of the situation."

"But why did she do it?" Kimberly asked.

"It is something I've been fearing for more than ten thousand years," Zordon said, his deep voice echoing in the room. "Rita has finally located the Power Eggs."

"The Power Eggs?" Zack said. "Uh, I don't get it."

"Me either," Jason said.

"Just look at the viewing globe and everything will become clear," Zordon said.

The Power Rangers gathered around a glass sphere. Images of

an ancient chest surrounded by ancient people appeared.

"Millions of years ago," Zordon said, "the war between Good and Evil began. So the good sorcerers hid a universe of power inside two special eggs. They put the eggs in a magic chest and threw the chest into the sea."

"But why?" Trini asked.

"The sorcerers believed that the Power Eggs would always be safe from evil forces there," Zordon said. "But just to make sure, they cast a spell. Only an innocent child could open the chest that holds the eggs."

"Is the chest still at the bottom of the sea?" Billy asked.

"No," Zordon said grimly. "It has washed ashore, into a slimy, dark, and dangerous cave."

"Oh, no," Kimberly said, pointing to the viewing globe. "Look!"

The Power Rangers peered into the globe. There they saw Maria, deep in the cave. The Putties surrounded her. Baboo was there, too. He was one of Rita's thugs. Together with the Putties, Baboo forced Maria to lift the magic chest and bring it to him. Then he made her open the chest. While two Putties held Maria, Baboo removed the Power Eggs and ran toward the entrance to the cave!

"We're wasting time!" Jason

shouted. "Let's go."

As the Power Rangers dashed out of the room, they heard Zordon's final piece of advice. "You must stand tall and prepare for battle."

The teenagers scrambled into the Rad Bug.

"Whoaaah!" they all yelled as Billy zapped them through space to the oceanside cave.

But when they arrived, they saw that Baboo and the Putties were not the only ones they would have to fight.

There was someone else—no, some*thing* else—waiting for them. One of Rita's monsters was standing at the entrance to the cave!

CHAPTER 6

The five teenagers climbed out of the Rad Bug. They bravely faced one of the most horrible monsters Rita had ever sent to Earth.

It was a seventy-foot-tall bird-like creature with terrible claws. Its beady eyes were blood red, and it had a razor-sharp beak. Rita called it the Hatchling!

The Hatchling and the Putties blocked the entrance to the cave where Maria was being held. There was no way for the teenagers to reach her.

Suddenly Baboo appeared from the cave holding the Power Eggs!

"Hold it right there!" Billy yelled. He reached into the Rad Bug and fired the cannon.

BOOM!

The force of the cannon blasted the Power Eggs from Baboo's paws. Like a rocket, the eggs sailed through the air and bounced over the edge of a cliff. Then they plunged into the icy ocean, hundreds of feet below.

From her fortress on the moon, Rita screamed.

"No!" she cried out. "My eggs!"

But the five friends didn't hear her. And even if they had, they wouldn't have cared. All they cared about right now was getting Maria back. But first they had to get past Rita's evil helpers.

Five Putties charged at them, but Baboo didn't stick around for the fight. He vanished in a puff of smoke.

"It's morphin time!" Jason cried out.

"Rangers, kick it!" Zack called.

"Let's do it!" Kimberly agreed.

The teenagers held their Power Morphers high. Just as Zordon had taught them, they called upon the spirits of the ancient dinosaurs.

"Mastodon!" cried Zack.

"Pterodactyl!" cried Kimberly.

"Triceratops!" cried Billy.

"Saber-toothed Tiger!" cried Trini.

"Tyrannosaurus!" cried Jason.

In a flash, five ordinary teens from Angel Grove morphed into— Power Rangers!

The five stood dressed as their super selves. Kimberly's outfit was bright pink. Trini's was yellow. Billy's was blue. Jason wore red and Zack wore black. They were now the most powerful fighting force on Earth.

The Power Rangers heard a screeching call. The Hatchling shot out a claw, and grabbed Maria from the cave!

"Let's get bird brain," Jason said. "But be careful—we don't want to hurt Maria!"

The Power Rangers raced into battle. They used all the karate moves they knew. The Putties gave up and ran away, but the Hatchling stayed right where it was.

"Look, the monster let go of Maria!" Kimberly yelled.

It was true. The Hatchling had put her down, so that it could fight with both claws. A terrified Maria ran and hid near the cave.

"Now that feather face will get what's coming to it!" Billy cried.

"I like my chicken stuffed!" Trini said, stomping on the Hatchling's toes.

The Power Rangers fought hard, but the Hatchling was winning.

Jason stopped fighting and raised his fist to the sky. "We need Dinozord Power!" he called to the others.

The Power Rangers quickly called out their dinosaurs' names. "Tyrannosaurus!" "Pterodactyl!" "Mastodon!" "Saber-toothed Tiger!" "Triceratops!"

Suddenly the ground trembled with the distant sound of dinosaur robots awakening.

Tyrannosaurus erupted from a steaming crack in the ground.

Mastodon broke through its cage of ice.

Triceratops charged across a scorching desert.

Saber-toothed Tiger leaped through a twisted jungle.

Pterodactyl erupted from the fires of a volcano.

Side by side the Dinozords raced like the wind to answer the call.

The Power Rangers leaped into the cockpits of their Dinozords. From the cockpit of his Dinozord,

Jason fired his weapons at the Hatchling. But no matter how many times he blasted the monster, it kept on fighting.

"What's with this creep?" Jason called. "I'm blasting it, and nothing works!"

The answer came from Zordon. His deep voice echoed into the cockpits of each of the Zords. "First you must destroy Romeo," Zordon said.

"Romeo?" Jason repeated. "Who's Romeo?"

"Romeo is the computer inside the Hatchling. It controls the beast."

"Do you know how to destroy it, Zordon?" Jason asked.

Zordon's mysterious answer was, "Be sure of yourselves and use your power."

Zack heard Zordon's words and thought about them hard. That's just what I told Cameron back at the youth center, Zack thought to himself. Cameron has to believe in himself—and so do we! "We need Megazord power!" cried the Black Ranger.

Jason thrust his fist into the air. "I call for the power of the Megazord!" he shouted.

Two Zords locked into a third, *Clunk! Clang!* and became legs. Two more Zords locked in, *Clang! Thunk!* and formed arms.

The mighty head rose from its

chest. Its helmet swung open and locked into place. Its shield clanged into its chest.

In moments the Dinozords had locked together to form the mighty Megazord!

Lights flashed on in the control room behind the Megazord's eyes.

Inside the Megazord, Jason sat at the controls, the other Power Rangers beside him. Jason blasted away at the Hatchling.

"Caw! Caw!" the monster screeched. It slammed its beak into the Megazord. The Megazord stumbled backward.

Now the Hatchling began to move. It trampled everything in its path. Even huge trees were smashed under its toes.

"There must be a way to destroy Romeo!" Billy shouted.

Suddenly Jason had an idea.

"I'm going inside the monster!" he called to the other Power Rangers.

"How are you going to do that?" Trini asked.

"The only way I know how," Jason cried. "The hard way!"

The Red Ranger jumped up. Bravely, he leaped out of the Megazord—and fell through space—right into the Hatchling's open mouth!

Inside the Hatchling everything was dark, wet, and slimy.

Jason looked around. Where
was Romeo? He figured that the
computer that controlled the
Hatchling should be somewhere
near its heart.

Jason remembered that Romeo

was a character in a famous play, *Romeo and Juliet.* "Romeo, wherefore art thou?" Jason called out, using a line from the play.

"Over here," a sickening voice answered. "Come closer, and you will meet your doom."

"Breaking your heart is more like what I had in mind," Jason said. He rushed toward the middle of the monster, and saw Romeo. It was a small box with blinking red lights and long cables coming from the top. But Romeo was ready for Jason. Quickly the computer wrapped Jason with strong cables. Jason was trapped! Zack called to Jason from the Megazord. "Jason, play the

Dragon flute!"

Jason struggled to reach for the Dragon flute in his pocket. The Power Rangers used it to call on the power of the Dragonzord. It was a special Zord, as big as the Megazord, with a powerful tail.

Jason kicked at the cables with all his might. Suddenly, a cable loosened. Jason grabbed the flute and quickly played a few notes. The Dragonzord appeared! It rose up in front of the Hatchling. It whipped its tail through the air and smashed it into the giant evil bird.

The force of the Dragonzord's blow knocked the wind out of the Hatchling. It also knocked the insides out of the Hatchling! All at once, Jason and Romeo came flying out of the big bird's mouth!

"Whooaaah!" Jason yelled as he hit the ground. Then he grabbed Romeo and disconnected it, once and for all!

In the next instant the Hatchling began to shake. Then it burst into thousands of feathers. Without Romeo the computer, the Hatchling could not survive. The feathers blew away and soon, there was nothing left.

"Morphinominal!" all the other Power Rangers shouted from the Megazord.

"Let's get Maria!" Trini and Kimberly said.

But first, the Power Rangers transformed back into teenagers.

Then Kimberly called out, "Maria, where are you? Are you okay?"

Maria ran from her hiding place and nodded. "Wow!" she said. "What an awesome day! I saw the Power Rangers!"

Kimberly and Trini laughed.

"That's what I like about you, Maria," Trini said. "You've got guts."

"Speaking of guts," Zack said, "let's go back to the gym to see how Cameron's doing in the karate match against Biff!"

With the help of the Rad Bug, the Power Rangers and Maria

were back at the youth center gym in seconds.

Inside, Cameron was lying on the mat, pinned down under Biff's enormous weight. But the look on his face showed he wasn't ready to quit.

"Cameron," Zack called, "use the new leg move!"

Cameron's eyes lit up when he heard Zack's voice. With a loud "Ki-yaaah!" Cameron used his leg to flip Biff off of him. Then he sprang into the air. He whirled and kicked, using karate and Hip-Hop-Kido moves! Then he landed at the end of the mat, facing the judges.

The crowd in the gym burst

into applause. A few minutes later, the head judge announced, "The winner is Cameron Haze!"

"Way to go!" Zack yelled, giving Cameron high-fives with both hands.

"Very impressive use of your musculature," Billy said.

"You were great," Trini agreed.

"But the important thing was that you believed in yourself," Zack said.

"Hey," Maria said. "Cameron was fun to watch, but can we go to the park now and finish our picnic?"

Kimberly and Trini rolled their eyes.

Kimberly said, "I think I've

maxed out on excitement for one day."

"But how about next week?" Trini suggested.

"Cool!" Maria said.

"But next time we have a picnic," Kimberly whispered to Trini, "I hope the fried chicken is the *only* bird that comes along!"